A DACHSHUND'S
WISH

A DACHSHUND'S
WISH

Joe Tavano

Illustrated by *Ji Yu*

TRAITOR DACHSHUND, LLC
NEW YORK

Traitor Dachshund, LLC
New York
www.traitordachshund.com

A Dachshund's Wish is a work of fiction. Names, characters, places, and events were created by the author. Any resemblance to actual events, places, or persons, living or dead, is purely coincidental.

Library of Congress Control Number: 2005908285

ISBN-10: 0-9744287-1-X
ISBN-13: 978-0-9744287-1-0

Published in the United States by Traitor Dachshund, LLC

Traitor Dachshund is a trademark and is a registered trademark of Traitor Dachshund, LLC

Printed in China

10 9 8 7 6 5 4 3 2 1

For my father

A DACHSHUND'S
WISH

PROLOGUE

Have you ever wondered what it would be like to be something else? Maybe a bird, so you could soar through the sky and explore our world from above? Or maybe a fish, so you could swim the oceans and discover the wonders down below? Well, our story is about just that. Humans aren't the only ones who wonder about being other things; animals do too. And when animals wonder, it's in a world that's far more different and magical than we could ever imagine. That's where our story begins.

CHAPTER 1

In a pet shop in Livingston, New Jersey, lay a red dachshund puppy in a cage behind a glass wall. His brother had left the day before and now he was alone. Only when he got up on his hind legs and leaned against the side of the cage could he talk to the old cat and the shaky Chihuahua. To make the time go by, he took a nap. He dreamed about his family on the farm—his brother; his mom, LeeAnn; and his dad, Bossy Joe. His mom said he was just like his dad. She'd find him in the afternoons hidden in a clump of dandelions, watching Emily the horse being brushed. In the fall, the farm was sold. LeeAnn and Bossy Joe moved with the family. The brothers were old enough to find new homes.

A tapping on the glass woke the puppy. He saw a boy smiling at him. He smiled back, got up, and started wagging his tail. This was the first time he was happy since leaving the farm and he felt a new life was about to begin.

"I want this one!" yelled the boy.

"I want this one!" the puppy barked.

"Dad, what kind of dog is that?"

"It's a dachshund, Jimmy."

His name is Jimmy, the dachshund thought.

"Can I have him, please, Mom, please, Dad?"

"Well, okay. But he has to be your responsibility," said his mom.

"And remember, Jimmy, you'll have to help more around the house. Wash the car with me. That was our deal," his dad said.

"I promise I'll do it," said Jimmy. "Can I pick him up?" And suddenly, the pet shop owner whisked the dachshund from his cage and the little dog landed in the outstretched hands of Jimmy.

"Paws! That's what I'm going to call you. Paws!"

Wow! I'm Paws! I've never had a name before. I'm somebody now! I'm Paws!

What more could a dachshund want?

Jimmy still held Paws close as he and his family left the store. It was a windy day and he didn't want Paws to be cold. When they got to the car, Jimmy's dad opened the back door and Jimmy, with Paws, got in.

"Everybody strapped in?"

Jimmy's dad started the car and they drove home, Jimmy and Paws hugging all the way. No sooner had the car stopped in the driveway, than Jimmy opened the door and he and Paws ran right onto the lawn.

Paws rolled over and over in the grass.

The feel of grass again!

When Paws got on his feet, he looked over his shoulder and gave Jimmy a big smile.

"Here, Paws." Paws ran to Jimmy.

"Mom, Dad, do you see how fast he is? I knew it."

Jimmy picked Paws up. "Here's your new home." They went in through the front door. Paws squirmed out of Jimmy's arms. He knew he needed to get right to work exploring. Because if a dachshund is going to do his job of protecting his new family, he has to be familiar with every sight, sound, and scent.

The family burst out laughing at the sight of Paws's nose going right into action. There was a familiar scent, very similar to Jimmy's. A girl came down the stairs.

Jimmy leaned toward Paws and whispered, "That's my sister, Donna. Don't get too close to her when she's playing with her dolls or she'll dress you up in one of their clothes." Paws didn't know what Jimmy meant, but he was happy to meet another member of his new family. He stopped exploring and ran up to Donna, wagging his tail. He sat down, barked, and stretched his head high. She reached to pet him.

"Aw, he's so cute. What's his name?"

"Paws," Jimmy replied.

"Welcome home, Paws. You'll play with me and my dolls."

"No, he won't," said Jimmy. "He's going to play catch with me and my friends."

Donna scratched Paws's ear and whispered, "Don't worry. We'll play dolls later."

Paws smiled and walked away. He still had more exploring to do.

I love my new family and I'm never going to let them down. Ever!

"Why don't you go to the car and get Paws the surprise we bought him?" said Jimmy's dad. Paws waited with big bright eyes for Jimmy to return. In a minute the front door banged open, and Jimmy stood there with something big in his arms. He came into the living room and put it down. Paws walked to it. It was a pillowy dachshund bed. His eyes welled with tears and he slowly made his way to the center of the bed, scraped a small flat area with his front paws, and lay down. He would never have to sleep in a cold, lonely cage again.

"Gee, look at that. What a smart dog! Can Paws sleep in my room? Please?" said Jimmy.

"Jimmy, Paws should stay downstairs for now until he gets familiar with the house," said his dad. "And later he can be in your room."

"Mom, please?"

"Your dad's right," his mom said.

"Okay." Jimmy bent down to hug Paws and whispered in his ear, "You'll be up in my room before you know it."

Jimmy carried Paws, still lying in his bed, over to the fireplace. Dad, Jimmy, and Donna went upstairs, and Paws saw Mom go over to a square on the wall. When she touched it, the house went dark. Paws put his head down between his front paws and took a deep, contented breath.

He thought about his old friends at the pet shop—the cat and the Chihuahua. He hoped they would find new families and that they would have big warm beds to sleep in. And as these thoughts ran through his mind, a quiet sense of love—the love of a family—filled the house. Paws's first day with his new family and his new home came to an end. And he began to dream as only a dachshund can.

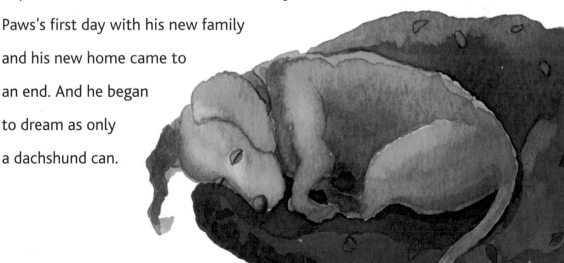

CHAPTER 2

The next morning Paws woke up to a delicious smell. He jumped out of his bed and ran toward the kitchen. His family was sitting at the table. Whatever was on that table made his nose twitch with delight.

"Good morning, Paws!" Mom said.

What a great morning greeting!

He made his way toward the table and sat by Jimmy's chair. Suddenly, Jimmy's hand dropped down in front of him, and there was something in it. Paws quickly snatched it, and something really tasty filled his mouth.

"Jimmy, I hope you're not sneaking Paws breakfast sausage. We don't want him developing any bad habits," Dad said.

Jimmy looked down at Paws, put his finger up to his mouth, and made a *shhhhhh* sound. Paws smiled and immediately ate another piece of sausage Jimmy smuggled down to him.

Gee, if I were a boy, I'd be able to sit at this table. Wouldn't that be grand?

But he was quickly distracted when Jimmy snuck him another piece of sausage.

When breakfast was over, Jimmy attached a leash to Paws's collar and said excitedly, "Come on, boy! Let's go to the park."

Wow, he called me a boy!

Jimmy opened the front door and came out with Paws happily by his side.

Paws put his nose to the ground. He loved smelling all the different scents of his new neighborhood, and his nose was certainly getting its share. There were many people and animals. There was plenty to see too. Each side of the street had a row of houses with big front lawns and shiny cars in the driveways.

After a few blocks, they got to the park. Jimmy ran toward two boys and Paws had no trouble keeping up.

"Hey, guys," Jimmy said. "Look at my new dog."

"Wow!" said Bobby. "He's cool. What's his name?"

"Paws," said Jimmy.

"You think Paws can play catch?" asked Joe, as he pulled out a rubber ball and threw it to Bobby. Bobby threw the ball to Paws, who caught it in his mouth and ran as fast as he could.

"Look at him go," said Bobby.

I could run even faster if I had two legs instead of four. And I could catch balls with my hands. And I could use a mitt, too.

But he stopped thinking about it because he was having too much fun.

It was getting late and Jimmy had to go home to wash his dad's car like he promised.

"Jimmy, let's play again tomorrow, and bring Paws. He's great," Bobby said.

Paws loved walking with Jimmy—it was so much fun keeping up. Again, he thought how the boys were able to run and jump using two legs. He tried lifting himself and walking on two legs. But after a few steps, back down he went on all fours.

"Wow, Paws, that's neat. Can you do it again?" asked Jimmy. Paws did his best but just couldn't walk more than a few steps on two legs. Jimmy didn't care; every time Paws tried, he'd laugh and hug his dog.

Paws was tired. When they got to the house, he lay down on the grass watching Jimmy help Dad wash the car. Paws shut his eyes and made a wish. A dachshund's wish. He wished he could be a boy. Just like Jimmy.

CHAPTER 3

After dinner when he went to his bed, Paws continued dreaming about being a boy. He was jarred awake by a noise coming from the basement. He didn't know what time it was but he knew it was late. His keen nose picked up the scent of strangers in the house.

"Hey, everyone, wake up!" he barked over and over again. Dad ran downstairs, turning on the lights. Mom, Jimmy, and Donna were close behind. Paws ran to the kitchen and stopped at the door, which led to the stairs to the basement. "They're down there! I smell them! They're right down there!"

Dad quickly put Paws on his leash and told Jimmy to hold him. He turned on the light and quietly opened the door to the basement and started down the stairs. The basement looked empty, and he breathed a sigh of relief. Then Dad noticed that the basement door was open. He always kept this door locked from the inside. It had been pried open. The molding was broken.

"Someone tried to break in." He grabbed the basement phone and dialed 911. "I'd like to report a break-in!" His voice trembled as he spoke.

Within minutes the police arrived. It didn't take them very long to come to the same conclusion.

"You were right, Mr. Jenkins. Burglars tried to get in," an officer said. "But all the noise this little guy here was making"—he pointed to Paws—"must have scared them away!"

"Paws!" Jimmy shouted. "You're a hero!"

Jimmy picked Paws up, and the whole family gave him a big hug. Paws didn't know what all the fuss was about. He was just doing a dachshund's job.

The officers finished up, said good night, and walked back to their patrol car. "They sure were lucky that little fellow had a big bark. I wouldn't have expected it from a dog so small."

The other officer smiled and said, "Well, you know looks can be deceiving."

The police officers got in their car and drove slowly, looking for any signs that other houses had been broken into. From the window the family watched and waved good-bye.

"Well, that was sure something. All right, the excitement's over," said Dad. "I think everyone should get back to bed. I'm going down to fix the basement door." As Dad went downstairs, Mom, Jimmy, and Donna said good night to Paws and they went to bed.

Later, Dad came up from the basement. He knelt next to Paws and patted him gently on the head. "Well, good boy, we certainly owe you one. I don't know what we would have done without you." He stood up, turned off the light, and went upstairs to bed.

The house was silent and dark and Paws went slowly back to sleep, knowing he had done a good job. He protected his family.

CHAPTER 4

Throughout the week Paws played basketball with Jimmy in the back-yard. Donna read Paws her favorite stories and they played dolls. And Mom and Dad were always generous with the treats when he was a good boy. Family life was more than just fun and games, though. After a couple of times of being naughty and chewing a hole in Mom's favorite blankets, Paws quickly learned there were rules.

Early one morning Paws woke up. Mom was in the kitchen preparing breakfast. Paws entered the kitchen and she said to him, "Why don't you go outside until breakfast is ready?" She opened the kitchen door and motioned to Paws to go down the stairs that led to the backyard.

He made his way down the stairs. Paws didn't notice the chill in the air because he was so busy exploring.

Under the big oak tree stood a most unusual creature.

"Hi! My name is Paws. And who are you?"

"I am Horatio, but around here they call me the Colonel."

"And what kind of creature are you?" asked Paws.

"I'm a hedgehog," he said. And he puffed out his chest.

A raccoon strolled around the trunk of the tree and a squirrel ran down the bark. "Paws," said the Colonel, "allow me to present Sadie the raccoon and my brave friend Sir Jonathan J. Squirrel."

"Nice to meet you both."

"I don't recall seeing you around these parts," said Sadie to Paws.

"Well, that's because I just arrived a week ago," answered Paws. "I belong to the family that lives here." Paws pointed to the house with his front right paw.

"Oh, so you're with those annoying humans who are always mowing their lawns," Jonathan grunted, remembering being chased off the grass when he was collecting nuts.

"Humans are not annoying," Paws quickly responded. "As a matter of fact I made a wish that I—" Paws couldn't continue.

"So, what was your wish?" asked the Colonel.

"You will all think I'm silly," said Paws.

"Don't be ridiculous! Tell us about your wish," demanded a curious Sadie.

"Well, if you really want to know, I wished I could be a boy." He stared up into the cloudy sky. "But I know that is just not possible."

"Why anyone would wish to be human is beyond me," the Colonel replied.

"But I really wish to be a boy."

"It's not enough to wish. You really need to *want* to be a boy," the Colonel said.

"I want to be a boy. I really want to be a boy."

"Well, if one did desire such change, only The Great Mae would have the power to make it happen."

Is it possible that somehow, someway, someone or something could make me into a boy? A real boy?

"Please, please tell me how I can find this Great Mae," implored Paws.

"The Great Mae can only be found if she wishes to be found," replied Sadie.

"I just know she'll grant my wish if I can find her. Please, you have to tell me where to go," begged Paws.

The Colonel's face grew very serious. "This is not for the weak. Finding The Great Mae is no easy task. If you wish to make this journey, it must start at dawn. And you must arrive at her place exactly two hours after sunrise, or you'll miss her and have to make the journey again."

"I can do it," insisted a very excited Paws.

"Then meet me here at zero six hundred hours sharp and I will set you on the path to meet her. Remember, time is critical, so you must not be late." The Colonel turned on his pads and marched off.

"What is zero six hundred hours?" asked Paws.

"That's why he's the Colonel." Jonathan the squirrel smiled. "It's military time."

"What does zero six hundred hours mean?" Paws asked.

"It means six o'clock in the morning," Jonathan said.

"I'll be here!" said Paws. He waved good-bye and ran back toward his house.

Could it be true that by this time tomorrow I could be a boy?

The thought was almost too much for him to bear.

The family was just sitting down for breakfast when Paws came up the stairs. He took his usual position on the floor next to Jimmy's chair.

After tomorrow I will be sitting in a chair at the table with my family. And then I will run on my two legs and catch a ball in my own hands. I'll have hands! Please, Great Mae, grant me this one and only wish!

As Jimmy's hand came down to sneak Paws some sausage, Paws prepared to live his last day as a dachshund. For tomorrow The Great Mae would surely make him a boy.

CHAPTER 5

As the sun broke from the horizon, Paws jumped out of his bed and ran toward the kitchen. "Somebody open the door! I've got to go meet the Colonel and The Great Mae!"

A very sleepy Jimmy made his way down the stairs and found Paws jumping and barking at the door. "You really need to go, huh?" Paws quickly squeezed out the barely open door and ran down the stairs.

Under the oak tree the Colonel was waiting for him. "You're right on time. That's good. You must not waste a second."

"I'm ready," exclaimed an excited Paws. "Tell me, sir, where will I find The Great Mae?"

"First you must find the rosebush. There is only one by the fence in the yard. When you get there, dig under the fence and that will get you into the woods."

"Digging under the fence will take hours. How can I possibly do it and still be on time?" asked Paws.

"Please don't interrupt me," snapped the Colonel. "Trust me. All things in life have a way of working out."

Paws needed to trust the Colonel if he was going to meet The Great Mae.

"Time grows short and there is much you need to know," said the Colonel. Paws's body grew rigid and he listened intently. "Once you've gotten under the fence you must go left and walk until you come to a tree with a bluejay's nest on one of its branches. There you will find a hollow log. You will have to walk through the log. This will be harder than it sounds and you will have to muster up all your courage. Are you following my directions, Paws?"

Paws's ears perked up. "Yes, I understand what you're saying."

"When you exit the log, continue on until you get to a brook. Then you have to cross over."

"But how will I cross the brook? I can't swim," Paws said.

"If you want to see The Great Mae, you have to find a way. After doing so, you will come to a horrible place, a metal graveyard. You will have to walk through this metal graveyard until you come to a large white-and-black rock. If you are on time, The Great Mae will make her appearance, give you an audience, and perhaps will grant your wish.

"Enough talk. Quick. Get going," the Colonel said. The hedgehog gave Paws a push forward, turned, and strutted off.

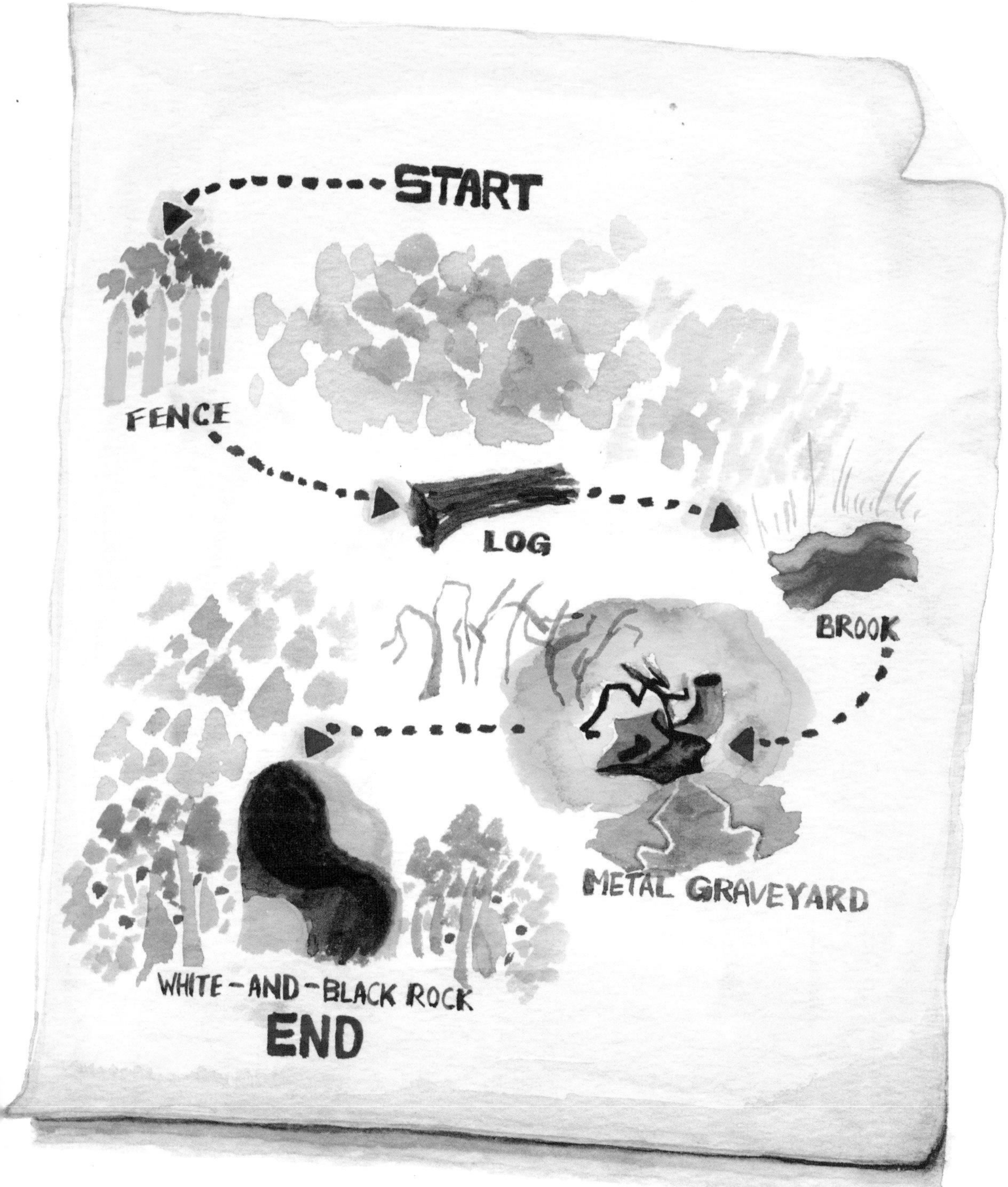
START
FENCE
LOG
BROOK
METAL GRAVEYARD
WHITE-AND-BLACK ROCK
END

"But how will I know who she is and what to do?"

The Colonel, not bothering to look back, said, "When the time comes, you will know what to do."

Paws took a deep breath and set out to find the rosebush. He didn't know how he was going to dig a hole big enough to get under the fence. But if he could dig the hole, there would be no turning back.

CHAPTER 6

Walking as fast as his dachshund legs could go, Paws made his way to the fence. The morning dew covered the grass and, being so low to the ground, Paws's chest got wet. He reached the fence and came up to the rosebush. He loved to dig, but how long would it take for him to make a hole to get under the fence?

He heard the sound of digging and went around the bush. A spray of dirt missed hitting him in the face.

What's going on here?

Then another batch of dirt whizzed by his head. He saw a big furry backside and a long striped tail. "Sadie! Is that you?" asked Paws. The digging stopped. Sadie wiggled out of the hole and turned to face the dachshund.

"Oh," she exclaimed, "you're here. Phew! I've been digging for hours."

"Why are you here?"

"Did you really think that you would be able to find The Great Mae without us helping you?" asked Sadie.

"You youngsters think you can take on the world by yourselves. Life would be very lonely and empty without our friends and family. And helping each other is what friends do." Sadie stepped aside to reveal a deep hole that she had been working on for the past few hours.

What a pleasant surprise!

What had appeared to be an impossible task for Paws just a few minutes before was now a path to make his wish come true!

A feeling overwhelmed him. It was the kind of feeling he had when Jimmy first held him in his arms in the pet shop. He wasn't quite sure how to describe it, but it was a feeling you get inside that makes you so warm that you smile as wide as your mouth can go. This wonderful creature with those incredible raccoon hands had just made the first part of his adventure easy. And Paws learned a most valuable lesson: Sometimes others are better able to deal with some of our obstacles in life. Sadie had dug the hole more quickly and deeply than he would ever have been able to do.

Paws said simply, "Thank you, Sadie." After a brief moment he added, "Thank you, my friend."

Sadie's face grew very soft. "All right." She could barely choke out the words. "Don't get all mushy on me and stuff. Come on! Get a move on. You don't want to be late, do you?"

Sadie's question made Paws afraid he'd be late and would miss meeting The Great Mae. "No, I can't be late. I have to get to The Great Mae on time. Good-bye," he said as he hunched down and ran through the hole. "The next time you see me I'll be a boy!"

Once he got on the other side of the fence, he could see that his journey through the woods was not going to be easy. It wasn't like the yard, all clean and open. These woods were just that—woods! Still, he was determined to find The Great Mae. His dachshund legs might be short, but they were strong. Following the Colonel's instructions, he proceeded left to his next landmark, the hollow log.

CHAPTER 7

The trees blocked the morning sun, making scary shadows all around Paws. He tried thinking of something else. Suddenly a familiar tune ran through his head. It was the song he heard Jimmy playing once while he was vacuuming the floor. Jimmy had taken his headphones off and put them over Paws's ears. It was that tune going through his head. It was Jimmy's favorite song! Paws remembered how much fun it was to wear Jimmy's headphones and watch Jimmy talk to him and not hear a word he said. It made Paws laugh. And now, with that music and wonderful memory, the walk wasn't so scary. His pace picked up. Maybe this wasn't going to be so bad after all.

In the distance, Paws saw up high in a tree a family of bluejays nested comfortably on a branch.

Sure enough, the Colonel was right. There was the hollow log.

He got to it and looked into the dark and musty log.

This is not a nice place! There are spiders and worms here. This is their home—not a very nice one, but still it's their home. How I wish I were home right now. The Colonel was right. This is going to take all my courage to get through.

The brave dachshund shook off his fears and the dampness of the woods. He was about to enter the log when he heard a strange voice say, "And where might you be headin', guv'ner?"

Paws peered around the side of the log and saw a large, scragglylooking gray rat leaning up against it. "Excuse me," said Paws. "Are you talking to me?"

"Me name's Rodchester," said the rat. "Rodchester Rodent."

"Nice meeting you, Mr. Rodent, I'm Paws. You speak very strangely."

"I'm English," replied Rodchester.

"Well, I speak English too, but not like that," said Paws.

"No, I'm from England," Rodchester said, surprised Paws didn't know. "Came over on one of those big boats docked in the seaport. I have to say, those boats are disgusting down below. Made me feel right at home."

Paws's face dropped. Dachshunds like things pretty clean. That's why the thought of going through this filthy log was not appealing to Paws at all. But Rodchester seemed right at home in this bug-infested place.

"So where ya headin', mate?" asked Rodchester again.

"I'm on my way to see The Great Mae. She's going to grant my wish . . . I wish I was a boy. And only The Great Mae is able to grant wishes. But she doesn't appear for very long, so I have to hurry . . ."

Grant wishes? thought Rodchester, as he tapped a finger on his lip. *If I could get to this Mae first, I could certainly keep her busy with my wish to have the biggest mound of cheese in the world.*

"So tell me, dog boy, how exactly are you going to get to this Mae?" Rodchester asked.

"Well," said Paws, "I'm already on my way. I have to go through this log, cross the brook, then pass through the metal graveyard and meet The Great Mae at the big white-and-black rock."

"White-and-black rock, eh?" The rat kept his thoughts to himself. *I'll get there before him and I'll be the richest rodent in the world. Now how do I get rid of this guy?* The corners of Rodchester's mouth perked up and a big evil smile grew over his face. *I know,* Rodchester plotted, *when this bloke goes into the log, I'll spin it around, and he'll come out right back where he started.*

"Sorry I don't have more time to talk with you, Mr. Rodent," said Paws. "I have to go."

"Why don't I keep you company, dog boy? I'll be right behind you," Rodchester said.

"Okay," said Paws, and he entered the log.

Now's my chance, thought Rodchester. He pressed as hard as he could against the end of the log. The log began to spin and Rodchester kept pushing until it was fully turned in the reverse direction. Off the rat ran, stealing Paws's chance to meet the Great Mae so he could become the richest rodent in the world. *Dog boy thinks he has to be in the log to meet the Bay or Hay or whatever that name was, but I know another way to get to the brook.* Rodchester laughed as he took a shortcut.

Paws was confused and disoriented.

Why is this log moving? Suddenly the log stopped. Paws got on his feet and as quickly as he could, ran through the wooden tunnel. When he came out, everything seemed exactly the same.

What's going on here? Am I right where I started?

He looked back.

And where's Mr. Rodent?

Paws quickly turned around and started through the log again and this time it didn't move. After about a minute, he came out of the log facing in the right direction. Rodchester was nowhere in sight. Paws grew angry.

Could Rodchester be on his way to The Great Mae to steal my wish and could he get there before me? I have to stop him!

Paws started running as fast as his short legs would take him. He had to get to The Great Mae first or his wish might not be granted. So on he went through the sticks, dirt, and twigs to the next landmark, the brook. He had to get across it, and he had to do it before that rat fink Rodchester.

CHAPTER 8

Paws remembered the cat in the pet shop telling him how fast rats were, so there was not a second to spare. Suddenly he came upon tall grass and knotted weeds. He looked both ways and saw that there was no way around it.

I have to get through this.

He walked right into it even though he might get lost. He tried to go fast, but his feet got tangled.

On the way back when I'm a boy I'll be walking through this with no problem!

This made him even more determined to get to The Great Mae first. He stiffened his body and put his head down and plowed right through the grass.

It seemed that as quickly as he got into the grass, he got out of it.

Wow! That wasn't so bad. Sometimes when things get a little rough, a little determination can go a long way. Good going, Paws! Now bring on that brook!

With the grass behind him, Paws felt like he could take on the world. He ran on.

He heard the sound of running water.

The brook!

He ran fast, *really* fast, just like he would run when he played ball with Jimmy and his friends—his tail bent, his body long, and his ears flapping in the wind! He was in a full-out dachshund run, making him feel so free and wonderful.

When Paws got to the brook, it was much bigger than he had imagined and he could see that getting across would take another miracle. He moved closer, right to where the grass met the water. He was pretty sure the water would be over his dachshund head.

Paws placed his paw over the edge. He shivered knowing he'd get so cold and wet crossing this brook. Paws leaned out farther and suddenly he lost his balance. And with a splash, he fell in.

"HELP! HELP ME!" he barked loudly. Thrashing around wildly, Paws was having trouble staying afloat. Water was getting in his eyes and it was becoming hard to see.

Oh no! I'm GOING UNDER!

He held his breath and felt nothing but water all around him. Then all of a sudden, something broke through the surface and came to rest in front of him.

Deep down inside Paws knew he was about to be saved.

With all his strength, he grabbed on to it with his dachshund mouth. It was furry and did not taste very good, but with a snap, he was pulled from the cold, murky water. It all happened so quickly. He was flipped in the air and ended up lying on the ground by the edge of the brook. Paws felt a blast of warm air on his body. He coughed up a little water and opened his eyes, and even though things were still out of focus, he saw the shape of something gray.

"Are you okay?" a voice asked.

I know that voice. But I can't see.

His vision cleared and he recognized Sir Jonathan J. Squirrel! It was his tail that had pulled him from the cold water.

"Oh, Sir Jonathan! You saved me! How can I ever thank you?"

"Easy now," said Jonathan. "You need to catch your breath."

"I tried to cross the brook, but I fell in," explained Paws as he closed his eyes and lowered his head. "How will I ever get across this thing? It's impossible!"

"So that's it?" said Jonathan. "You're going to give up just like that?"

"Well, what can I do?" asked Paws. "I can't walk across it."

"Walk across, huh?" Jonathan's eyes widened and he smiled. "That's exactly what you're going to do, Paws. Walk right across! Let's go."

Paws followed the squirrel downstream but couldn't imagine what Jonathan was talking about.

"Where are we going?" Paws asked.

"We are going to make you into a boy," said Jonathan. "That's where we are going! So hurry and just keep up!"

Jonathan ran up to an animal with a big, wide, strange tail. Paws had

never seen anything like him. "Let me introduce my good friend," said the squirrel as Paws came up to them. "This is Barton the beaver."

"Hello, Paws-s-s," said Barton. "It's-s-s a pleas-s-sure to meet you."

He had the biggest front teeth Paws had ever seen! "S-s-s-o, what brings-s-s you here?"

"Well," said Jonathan, "Paws needs to cross this brook."

"Why would he want to go to the other s-s-side?" asked Barton.

"He's on his way to meet The Great Mae," said Jonathan.

"I want to be a boy," said Paws.

"Well, if anyone can help you, Paws-s-s, it's-s-s The Great Mae," said Barton.

How could this creature possibly help me cross the brook? I guess if he lives here, he must be a good swimmer. But Barton's back certainly can't be strong enough to give me a ride. And, even if he could, I'd still get wet and cold again.

"Come with me," said Barton, and Paws and Jonathan followed. Paws could see other beavers hard at work on something. Whatever it was, it stuck out from the surface of the brook.

"This is the most amazing construction," said Paws, looking at the thick wall stretching across the brook. It looked like it was made of mud, sticks, and all sorts of other things from the woods, holding the water back. The other side was dry. Well, not completely dry, but certainly dry enough for him to walk across.

"I told you that you were going to walk right across, and that's just what you're going to do," declared Jonathan.

Paws's face lit up with excitement! With the help of Jonathan and his new friend Barton, he was going to cross this brook!

"That's a wonderful wall, Barton," exclaimed Paws.

"It's-s-s a dam," said Barton, holding a stick in his hand and pointing to the dam. "We beavers-s-s make dams-s-s out of branches-s-s. The dams-s-s are our homes-s-s, where we live. Making dams-s-s comes naturally to us-s-s."

"Well, Paws," interrupted Jonathan. "You had better get going."

Paws carefully walked down into the brook bed. "Thank you both for your help."

"Remember, Paws," Jonathan shouted. "There is always a way to solve a problem! Sometimes the answer lies in what seems to be beyond your means. But there is always an answer. You just need to find it!"

"Yes," replied Paws. "I will remember that always!"

He walked for a few steps and then stopped quickly. He turned, looked back, and asked, "Hey! By the way, you guys didn't happen to see a rat come by here, did you?"

They both shook their heads, puzzled.

"Oh, never mind," Paws said under his breath as he proceeded to do the impossible. He was crossing the brook and on his way to see The Great Mae.

CHAPTER 9

Paws got to the other side of the brook and walked up the embankment. He peered over the edge and got an eerie feeling. The world on this side of the brook was very different from where he lived. The earth was dry and stained with shades of orange and black. Plants and trees were brown and dead. The air smelled of corroded metal.

Paws climbed over the embankment and he looked over his shoulder. His friends, the squirrel and the beaver, were on the other side. How he wanted to be there with them right now.

This is not such a nice place.

The landscape was lifeless and the soil was brown, dried, and cracked. And streams of orange ran down toward the brook.

What caused this?

Then it hit him. This was the metal graveyard, the horrible place the Colonel said he'd have to go through.

Paws was overwhelmed with loneliness. This place was totally barren with nothing but discarded metal machinery and garbage as far as his dachshund eyes could see. "What happened to this place?" Paws said out loud.

"It was the humans," replied a voice. Paws looked up and saw a blackbird sitting on an old, rusted, decaying washing machine. "This place was once full of life like the other side of the brook," said the blackbird. "I've lived here for many years and watched them dump their garbage here." Paws looked around and saw old broken cars, televisions, and refrigerators. "The rust and debris from their garbage seeps into the earth every time it rains. That is what killed this place." The blackbird grew silent.

"Why would they do such a thing?" asked Paws. "How could anyone want to do such a terrible thing?"

The blackbird flew off the washing machine and landed next to Paws. "Humans sometimes forget they share this place with other creatures," the blackbird said. "This was once home to many of the animals in these woods. But they're not here anymore."

Paws looked around and could not even imagine this land ever being home to anything or anyone.

Mr. Blackbird can't mean everyone is like that. My family isn't like that.

"I am very sorry." Paws and Mr. Blackbird stood quietly and watched as the wind forced a dented oil can to roll toward the brook.

"Maybe you can help me. I am looking for a large white-and-black rock in this area. Do you know where it is?"

"Ah, so you seek The Great Mae," replied the blackbird.

"You know of her?" asked Paws.

"Many seek, but few find," said the blackbird. "She will only appear to those who truly deserve her powers. Those who are good and pure of heart. The rock you seek is just beyond this place." He pointed his beak toward a gutted car. "But be careful," he continued. "There are many pits in the ground here. You wouldn't want to fall into one."

"Thank you for your help, Mr. Blackbird." Paws walked toward the car. "I will be careful."

Suddenly Paws picked up an awful scent. "Where have I smelled that before? Rodchester!" He carefully peered around the side of the car and saw a large hole in the ground.

"'Ey, guv'ner." A voice came from down in the hole. "Want to lend a hand?"

"Lend you a hand? After what you did to me!" Paws said, coming out into the open. "You've got some nerve!"

"Come on now. Can't you Yanks take a good joke?" said Rodchester. "I was going to get there and make sure your Bay friend would wait for you."

"Mae," replied Paws, as he walked closer to the hole. "Her name is The Great Mae."

"Come on, get me out of here. Look at what I did for you. I saved you from falling into this hole," shouted Rodchester.

Gee, maybe I should help him. But if I let him out, he'll just try to steal my wish again. Maybe for the time being he's right where he should be, out of trouble.

"I will come back to rescue you later after my wish is granted," Paws shouted into the hole.

"You can't just leave me here, mate," the rat shouted back.

"Oh, yes I can," said Paws. "At least I know where to find you."

Paws walked around the hole and on to his final destination: the large white-and-black rock. He was finally going to meet The Great Mae.

CHAPTER 10

In the distance Paws saw grass, green lovely grass. His pace picked up. The grass felt so good to walk on, not dry and bumpy.

Trees! Trees with large branches and bright green leaves!

The farther he went, the more beautiful things became. Paws thought for a moment about how terrible a place the world would be without the beauty of grass, trees, and flowers.

Paws saw the white-and-black rock growing in size with each step he took. He was getting closer and his heart raced. Paws was overwhelmed with the excitement of meeting The Great Mae. Before he knew it, he was at the rock. He felt a great sense of pride. All his hard work and determination was about to pay off.

The white-and-black rock was oval with a cutout in the middle. It looked like the big plush chair in his family's living room.

A dense patch of very tall yellow grass was behind it.

He lifted his head to the sky, and the sun was at eight o'clock. He was right on time. Now the only thing missing was The Great Mae. He sat down on his tired hind legs.

I bet the family is having breakfast now. I miss them.

He thought about all the fun he had when Jimmy snuck him food at the table, and how everyone stopped whatever they were doing and took a moment to pet his head and back. He loved being told he was a good boy. But, of course, there was that time he grabbed Donna's doll in his mouth and ran away with it. He got in so much trouble he was sent to his bed. That wasn't so much fun. But right now he'd welcome a nice long nap in that very bed.

His dachshund ears perked up. The tall grass rustled from behind the rock. "This is it," he said. "She's here! The Great Mae has arrived." He stood up on his four legs as straight as he could.

How disrespectful would it be to greet such nobility sitting down? And what type of creature could The Great Mae be? Whatever she is, she will have the look of royalty, with the wisdom of an owl and the power of a mare, like my old friend Emily the horse on the farm.

The sound grew louder. He felt like his heart was about to break through his dachshund chest. His eyes opened really wide, and he couldn't help but smile. He could almost hear the sound of trumpets in his head announcing the arrival of The Great Mae.

At that very moment, a little orange head popped through the tall grass. The smile on Paws's face instantly dropped and the trumpet playing ended with a sour note. He stared in disappointment as an orange body followed that head out of the grass. It was a tabby cat. A common, mangy, and in this case, flea-bitten tabby cat.

Paws looked around it to see if The Great Mae had gotten stuck behind this cat trying to make her entrance. But no. No one else was coming out of the grass. Paws sat back down and figured that he would need to wait a little longer for The Great Mae to arrive.

The cat walked over and sat down right in front of Paws. Paws got a little annoyed at that, because the cat was blocking his view of the big white-and-black rock. The tabby chuckled. "What's so funny?" asked Paws.

"Forgive me. I didn't mean to laugh, but I was admiring that long body of yours. It is quite unusual," said the gentle feline. "And what brings you to this neck of the woods?"

"Well, if you must know," replied Paws, "I am here to meet The Great Mae." He really had no interest in carrying on a conversation, but figured until The Great Mae arrived he would chat politely.

"And exactly what have you heard about this Great Mae and why do you wish to have an audience with her?" asked the cat.

"If you don't mind, I'd rather just tell my story to her," replied Paws.

"Well, as you can see, it is only the two of us here so far," said the tabby. "So keep an old cat company and tell me what brings you here."

There was no getting rid of this old cat, so Paws decided to tell the tabby what it wanted to hear. Besides, the time would go quicker.

"I am Paws and live with my family on the other side of the brook. I have but one wish. And I was told that by coming here The Great Mae could make my wish come true."

"And tell me, young Paws," said the tabby cat, "exactly what miracle do you wish The Great Mae to perform?" The cat looked deeply into Paws's eyes. For a scrappy old cat it had a powerful stare.

Paws began to feel almost hypnotized and lay down with his head up to tell the rest of his story. The tabby lay down too. Paws looked around and even though The Great Mae was not in sight, he somehow knew she was listening.

CHAPTER 11

The morning air grew warmer and the sun shone through the clouds on Paws and the tabby cat.

Why won't this cat leave?

As he lay there Paws thought about his family's yard. He found a favorite rock and he would lay and sun himself for hours. The warmth of the sun always felt so good on his face.

"So, Paws,"—the voice broke into his daydream—"what will you ask of The Great Mae?" asked the tabby cat again.

"I want her to make me into a boy," replied Paws.

"That's a pretty tall order for anyone to perform," said the tabby. "Are you sure The Great Mae is able to do something like that?"

And who are you to question the powers of The Great Mae? How could such a simple orange tabby cat possibly understand what is about to happen here?

"I don't expect someone like you to understand," said Paws. "What The Great Mae and I will be doing is way above the head of a common tabby cat."

The comment didn't seem to bother the cat, and the tabby went on to ask, "Well then, humor me and tell me why you wish to become a boy."

"The family that adopted me is the most wonderful family anyone could want," said Paws. "And Jimmy is my best friend. We go everywhere and do everything together. We play all the time, and I help him with the chores. Well, actually Jimmy does the chores. I sort of supervise." Paws thought of Jimmy vacuuming while he chased and barked at the vacuum cleaner. "I want to be able to sit and eat breakfast at the table with the family," Paws continued. The big tabby cat sat listening.

"But you know what?" Paws said slowly. "It wouldn't be as much fun. I'd miss Jimmy sneaking food to me, then putting his finger to his mouth, telling me to keep quiet. We got such a laugh out of that. It was our little secret."

"Sounds to me like you had a lot of fun with Jimmy," said the cat.

"That's only the beginning." Paws stood up. "We'd go to the park together and meet Bobby and Joe. We played catch and when they threw me the ball, I'd grab it in my mouth and take off! Then they would chase me. It was so much fun. I would always let Jimmy catch me. He would fall down in the grass next to me and laugh so hard as he tried to take the ball from my mouth. I never gave it up easily. But in the end, I always let

Jimmy have it."

Paws lay down again. "Gee, I guess when I become a boy, playing catch won't be as much fun anymore. I really liked being chased. But I'll be able to catch the ball in my hands and run on two legs. It'll be just as much fun."

The cat looked closely at Paws and raised one eyebrow.

"It will too," Paws insisted.

"You tell of wanting this transformation, yet it sounds like life as a dachshund suits you. You still haven't given me a good reason to—"

"You just said 'me,'" interrupted Paws. "Why did you just say 'me'?"

The cat didn't answer Paws's question. Instead, she said, "Paws, what was that one really important time with your family?"

Paws knew. He didn't even have to think about this one. "The night the burglars broke into our house. I heard them, but no one else did. I made so much noise that everybody woke up and ran downstairs and the robbers ran away."

"Paws. What do you think would have happened if you were not there that night?"

"Well,"—Paws thought for a moment—"I guess those bad men would have robbed my family."

"Oh, Paws," said the tabby, "the robbers would have gone upstairs looking for money and Jimmy's father would have tried to stop them. There would have been a fight. Your being there changed everything." The cat's face grew grim. "If it hadn't been for your keen senses, your family would have been hurt."

"How do you know that? How do you know what would have happened to them?"

The cat continued. "And remember the officers that night, Paws?"

"Yes, I do. There were two of them," Paws said.

"Well, when they were leaving one of them said he was surprised that a dog as small as you had such a big bark," said the cat.

"Really?" Paws didn't think of himself as small.

All of a sudden the tabby looked different. Her orange coat appeared thick and shiny. As she rose, she stood tall. Her face, no longer old and shabby, looked beautiful and wise. The cat walked over to the large white-and-black rock and sat on it as though it were a big comfortable chair.

Or a throne.

Paws watched the cat sit down with her new look of royalty.

"I know these things, Paws, because I am the one you seek. *I* am The Great Mae," proclaimed the cat.

In the blink of an eye Paws was face-to-face with the creature he had worked so hard to meet.

CHAPTER 12

"**G**reat Mae, it is such an honor to be in your presence," declared an excited Paws.

"Ah, so *now* it is an honor, but just five minutes ago I was an annoying old cat to you," said a not-so-amused Mae.

"I didn't know—" Paws tried to apologize, but The Great Mae interrupted him.

"Let this be a lesson to you, Paws. All creatures deserve respect. We should not judge anything or anyone by appearances. Appearances can be deceiving. It is what is inside each of us that makes us great. Just because I did not appear to you as you expected did not give you the right to treat me differently. I tested you to see if you deserved the gift of a wish. So tell me, Paws, why should I grant one to you?"

Gee, it's true, I wasn't so nice to The Great Mae. I looked at the outside and not what really counts.

"You're right. I guess I don't deserve a wish after the way I treated you. All I can ask is for you to forgive me and I will be on my way and not bother you anymore." Paws lowered his head.

"I know of your travels here. I know how you almost drowned in your quest to find me. You faced your fears and overcame all obstacles. You believed I could make you a boy. And yet you're ready now to walk away from your wish in return for forgiveness." The cat smiled. "That is a great quality."

Paws looked into the eyes of the cat, only this time he saw what was inside—all the wisdom and kindness of which The Great Mae was capable.

"I will grant you your wish, Paws."

Paws's tail started to wag. This was it! He was going to be a boy. He was going home a boy. He would sit at the table next to Jimmy and eat with the family. He would catch a ball in his hands. And he'd have two legs to run and jump.

Out of the corner of his eye Paws saw his tail wagging wildly. He remembered the sound it made when it beat against something. And how whenever he was bored, he'd play a game to try to catch it. And he remembered how much Jimmy loved that tail of his. It let everyone know how happy he was.

Boy, am I going to miss not having that tail.

"Are you having second thoughts?" asked the tabby. The Great Mae knew he was struggling.

"Uh, no Great Mae. I'm okay. I'm ready." The dachshund closed his eyes. "Yes, I'm really ready. Please make my wish come true. Please make me a boy!"

Paws waited to feel something happen.

This is really strange. Shouldn't I be feeling my two legs grow?

He peeked open one eye to look. That tail of his was still there and he was still standing on four legs.

"Did you think it was going to be that easy?" asked the cat, as she let out a good hearty laugh. Paws didn't understand what was so funny.

"This dramatic change requires more than just closing your eyes," said The Great Mae. "There is a catch. The price you will pay for being a boy is that you will not be a boy with Jimmy and his family. You will eat at a table, you will catch a ball in your hands, and you will run and jump on two legs. But you will not do it with them."

"And what will happen to Jimmy?" asked Paws.

"Well, from Jimmy's point of view, you just left one morning and never came home," said The Great Mae. "He will search for you, his best friend, for months, but he will never find you. He will never know why you left or what happened to you. Your wish, unfortunately, will leave him and his family heartbroken. Remember, they love you."

"Life without Jimmy and his family?" Paws never thought that being a boy meant he'd never see his family again. He may have wanted to be a boy, but he wanted to be a boy with them. And just the thought of Jimmy being hurt by his wish—well, nothing was worth that!

"Well, Paws," said The Great Mae as she got up from her throne. "Are you ready? Are you ready to become a real boy?"

A look of distress came over Paws's face. He backed away from The Great Mae. He didn't want it anymore. He didn't want to be a boy. He just wanted to be back with Jimmy and his family. Suddenly catching a ball with hands didn't matter. What did matter was seeing Jimmy's smiling face. Getting a pat on the head from Dad and hearing "good boy." Smelling Mom's delicious breakfast. And getting hugs from Donna.

"No!" shouted Paws. "No, I'm not ready! Great Mae, I'm so sorry to have wasted your time, but I no longer wish my wish. I'm happy being just me. I don't want to be anything else! My wish now is to go home to my family as me, Paws, the dachshund. I want to have Jimmy sneak me food again. I want to catch a ball in my mouth. I want to run on all four legs, and I want to keep my tail! Just as long as I can do it all with Jimmy!"

The Great Mae softly smiled. "That's one wish I don't need to grant you, Paws. It has been yours all along. Now go, go back to your family. Jimmy is so worried about you and misses you terribly. Run home and don't waste any time. Your family is waiting for you."

"You've shown me so much," replied a happy Paws. "I am so grateful to you for granting me the greatest wish of all. You gave me . . . ME! Good-bye, Great Mae, and thank you," Paws said as he started off to a whole new life.

"Oh, one other thing, Paws," said The Great Mae. Paws stopped immediately. "You may tell of meeting me, but you must not tell what I looked like. I can appear differently to everyone. Others who seek me must be tested too. These things must remain a secret."

"Don't worry. Your secret is safe with me," exclaimed a very excited

Paws. A disturbing thought crossed his mind. "Rodchester! I promised I'd rescue Rodchester."

"I will take care of Rodchester. You just get on your way home now," said The Great Mae with a not-so-happy look at having to deal with that rat.

Without a second thought, Paws took off, his heart pounding faster and faster. He was on his way home. He was on his way to Jimmy.

CHAPTER 13

Exhausted, Paws kept running. His best friend was waiting for him, and he didn't want him to worry anymore.

Was this a dream?

Running through the metal graveyard, he looked straight ahead.

Rushing to the brook, he quickly crossed the top of the beavers' dam. When he got to the hollow log, he ran alongside instead of through it.

Never know if Rodchester is around.

He got to the hole that Sadie the raccoon had dug. He stopped for a minute.

Wow! This is where it all began. It really wasn't a dream. It did happen!

Paws closed his eyes and made his way through the hole under the fence. Coming out of the hole and opening his eyes, he saw a big surprise. There in the yard were all his friends. Barton and the other beavers from the brook, Mr. Blackbird from the metal graveyard, Sadie the raccoon, Jonathan the squirrel, and the Colonel.

"Welcome home!" said the Colonel. Paws's tail was going a mile a minute.

"I see you're still a dachshund." Sadie smiled.

"Yes, Sadie, I'm still a dachshund. I met The Great Mae—" The crowd let out an "oohhhhhhhhhh." "She was everything you said she would be. She was so wise. She did grant me a wish, even if it wasn't the one I thought I wanted."

"I'm so glad you're still you," said Jonathan. "We all hoped you would return to us just the way you were. And you did!"

The crowd let out a heartfelt "Welcome home, Paws!"

Paws was deeply touched by this wonderful reception. Yet he heard an unmistakable voice come from within the crowd, a voice that made him cringe!

"'Ey, mate. Hope you're not too upset about the log thing." It was Rodchester the rat.

Paws was even glad to see him. "What are you doing here?" he asked.

"Aw, some mangy old cat made me promise to come here or it was going to leave me in that hole."

The Great Mae.

In the distance Paws saw the silhouette of a cat sitting in the oak tree. Its tail was hanging down, moving slowly back and forth. Paws couldn't fully see her face, but he somehow knew The Great Mae was watching.

A warm, comfortable feeling came over him. He had met The Great Mae and had wonderful friends who would always be there for him. And he would always be there for them. He would never be alone.

"Jimmy!" he suddenly said out loud. "I need to see Jimmy now! Thank you all for everything you've done." Paws's eyes grew misty. "Mostly, thank you for being my friends. This will always be the greatest day of my life. And you all made it possible."

"I saw Jimmy looking for you," said the Colonel. "He was very worried. I think he was crying. He needs you now." The figure in the tree nodded in agreement.

"I must leave you," said Paws. "It's time for me to see my best friend in the whole wide world. It's time for me to see Jimmy."

Paws took off like a rocket toward the house as the group waved and said good-bye to him. "Welcome home, my boy," the Colonel quietly said to himself as he watched Paws run toward his house. This time, Paws was here to stay.

Paws went around the garage and ran up the stairs leading to the kitchen door. He began to bark. "Jimmy! It's me, Paws! Open the door,

Jimmy. It's me! I've come home. Please open the door!"

All of a sudden the door swung wide open and there on the other side stood Jimmy. Paws excitedly barked, "Jimmy!" as Jimmy yelled, "Paws!" at the same time. Jimmy bent down, and Paws ran to him and lifted himself up, resting his front paws on Jimmy's shoulders. Paws couldn't stop licking Jimmy's face.

"I was so worried about you, boy! Where did you go?" Jimmy kept hugging Paws. They felt each other's hearts beating. They couldn't let go of each other.

The family joined Jimmy in the kitchen.

"He's home!" shouted Jimmy.

"Look, Paws finally

came home!"

Dad walked over to Paws, picked him up under his front legs, and looked him in the eye. "You gave us all quite a bit of worry, young man." He put Paws back on the floor and continued, "But it's good to have you back." Then came the words Paws longed to hear from Dad. "You're a good boy!"

Mom and Donna rushed over to Paws. This time there were more than just hugs from Donna. She was so happy to see him that she bent down on her knees and kissed Paws on the top of his head.

Paws looked over to Mom and saw a look of happiness and love. In her eyes Paws could see that The Great Mae was right. This was his family.

Jimmy put down a big bowl of water, and Paws took a much-needed drink. Worn out from his adventure, he looked for his bed by the fireplace, but he didn't see it.

"You must be really tired, Paws. Come with me," said Jimmy. Paws followed him upstairs. As Jimmy opened his bedroom door, Paws's eyes grew wide and his tail stood still. He couldn't believe what he was seeing. Jimmy had placed Paws's bed next to his own.

"I had to promise Mom and Dad I'd help Donna with her homework before they let me bring your bed up here," said Jimmy. "So what are you waiting for? Get in!"

Paws walked over to it, climbed in, and, as always, scraped a little flat area and lay right down. Jimmy sat down on the floor and watched over him. Paws looked at Jimmy, feeling safe and warm.

Now I can always be by Jimmy's side.

He fell asleep. Jimmy saw Paws's eyes moving under their lids. His paws started to twitch, and his tail was moving, too. Then he surprised Jimmy by letting out a little "woof."

It was clear that just like a boy, Paws was dreaming. And he dreamed, as only a dachshund could dream.

JOE TAVANO created *A Dachshund's Wish* by drawing on the reactions of his own dachshund—Paws, of course—to the wild animals he encountered in his suburban backyard. *A Dachshund's Wish* is Tavano's first children's book and a wild departure from his usual activities. A graphic designer and videotape editor, Tavano works in edit suites to create audio and video programming for broadcast and cable television clients such as Nickelodeon, NBC, and Spike TV.

A strong supporter of animal welfare, Tavano designed the 2004–2005 Rescue Dachshund Pin (www.rescuedachshund.com). The Pin is a creative, nationwide rescue-awareness campaign that funds the medical expenses incurred by the Almost Home Dachshund Rescue Society (AHDRS) and its dachshunds in "foster care." Each annual Pin illustrates the experience of a particular AHDRS rescue dog.

Tavano hopes children learn from Paws that humans and animals share love and dreams. He lives in New York City.

Ji Yu holds a Bachelor of Fine Arts degree from Rhode Island School of Design, a Master of Fine Arts degree from Hunter College in New York City, and has studied in Paris and Rome. *A Dachshund's Wish* is the first book she has illustrated. In developing the pencil and watercolor drawings for this book, Yu revisited her own childhood and tried to see the story through the eyes of a little girl. "I used to look at all the pictures before I read anything, and I tried to imagine what I'd like to see if I read this story as a child." Yu teaches in the art departments of George Washington University and Montgomery College. She and her husband live in Vienna, Virginia.